THE
DARK QUEEN

The Dark Queen
A Supernatural Short Story
Copyright © J.F.Penn (2017, 2019). All rights reserved.

www.JFPenn.com

ISBN: 978-1-912105-30-4

Requests to publish work from this book should be sent to:
joanna@CurlUpPress.com

Cover and Interior Design: JD Smith Design

Printed by Amazon KDP

www.CurlUpPress.com

THE
DARK QUEEN

A SHORT STORY

J.F. PENN

"Come on, Mark." I smile up at him with a hint of flirtation. "Just one more dive. I won't be long."

Mark, the Dive Crew Manager for the day, looks up at the darkening sky.

Clouds gather above the port of Alexandria in the distance, a bruised vortex against the minarets of the city. Water slaps roughly on the hull. The wind picks up, the sea louder now as the turquoise Mediterranean turns to violet capped with white foam. A chill sweeps around the boat, hunting for cracks to force itself into. I shiver, pulling up my wetsuit to cover goose-pimpled flesh. The smell of decomposition wafts on the wind, dead things and offal from the rubbish barges near the shore, a stagnant rotting fish odor that makes my nose crinkle.

It's been a backdrop to the summer, but I'm still not used to it, even now.

"Storm's coming." Mark looks at his watch. "It's almost the end of shift and the other boats have all headed back. Besides, you don't have a buddy. Frank's changed and sleeping down below."

Desperate thoughts run through my mind.

But I have to go down before the storm comes, before the silt of the seabed covers the city.

I saw something down there. The Dark Queen. I'm sure of it.

I need–

"I'll go with her."

His voice is like the edge of the abyss, a smooth oblivion that beckons to the depths. Seductive. Dangerous.

Khalid leans against the side of the boat, wetsuit half-peeled off revealing his lean torso, muscles taut and powerful, a threat made flesh. His dark eyes flash to mine.

"I'll take you down."

My mind flashes back to that night in Alexandria when the archaeological team first met for the season. He was charming at first, but he changed when we were alone. The marks on my wrists had taken weeks to fade, the bruises on my thighs ached and I had bled inside. He had laughed at my tears, confident of his position on the team. He was the main Egyptian cultural liaison, a key part of the dive expedition, and I … well, I needed to be on this trip. I'd been a junior on too many digs and my grant was over unless I could prove myself valuable this time.

Whatever the cost.

With careful management, I'd managed to avoid diving with him as a buddy, even making sure I was on a different boat most days as the excavations progressed. But today …

I need to go down there. If I find the Dark Queen …

I clench my fists and nod slowly, looking back at Mark. His decision would be final.

He nods. "Alright, but you only have thirty minutes bottom time. No longer. I mean it, Lara."

Khalid and I gear up next to each other, both of us used to the rhythm of the dive boat, both experienced divers with years of underwater archaeology between us, but my hands still shake.

He brushes my arm. I flinch away and a smile lifts the corner of his mouth.

"Which quadrant do you want to search?"

I grab the waterproof chart printed with the layout of the drowned city beneath us, holding it out in front of me, a barrier between our bodies.

"Here, between the Temple and the cemetery."

Khalid stops checking his gear and leans closer. "You seek the Dark Queen?" His voice is almost a whisper, less confident now, and there is hesitation in his eyes.

I nod. "What do you know of her?"

He looks back towards Alexandria in the distance, the edge of a country layered by myth and brutal history.

"Legend tells of a powerful Queen of this

city who ripped men apart to avenge an ancient wrong. When the streets ran thick with blood, the people called for justice. The greatest magician in Egypt trapped the Queen inside a statue and flooded the city to keep her eternal rage captive."

My thoughts race at his words. I hear her calling to me, as she has done every night since we started diving here.

I sense his hesitation and tilt my head to one side, eyes fixed on his, daring to challenge him. "So you don't want to come, then?"

He shrugged. "It's just a legend." He leaned closer. "I wouldn't miss going down with you." He pulls a heavy dive knife out of its sheath with a rasp and checks the blade for nicks. He holds it casually, the knife edge towards me for a pointed second, then he thrusts it back into the sheath and attaches the weapon to his calf with its rubber strap.

Gearing up quickly, Khalid steps off the back of the boat into the choppy waves. I see dark shapes shift in the waters beneath him, shadows with teeth and tentacles waiting for prey to step into their domain.

"You going then?"

I blink and the images fade. Mark notes the time as I step into the water with a splash and swim over to Khalid, pushing away thoughts of what might be below. We both give the OK signal before sinking beneath the water.

It's dark below as the storm grows overhead and the cold penetrates my wetsuit immediately, the chill of the dead city wrapping around us. We turn on powerful torches and descend towards the ruins of what was once Egypt's greatest port. Thonis-Heraklion disappeared from history two thousand years ago, and was only rediscovered this century, a perfectly preserved ancient city buried under the silt of the Mediterranean. Archaeological dive teams cleared away much of the seabed that covered it, but as the summer season draws to a close, there is still so much left to uncover. I don't want to leave. Here is history and my place in it.

Equalizing and finding neutral buoyancy, we

fin along the sea floor. I can hear the rhythmic sound of my breath and the bubbles of exhalation, the click of fish feeding. The water is full of silt, an eerie green of hanging particles that refract the light and make shadows seem much larger.

The colossal head of a god emerges from the gloom, hacked from its torso and decapitated on the sea bed, its sightless eyes staring into the deep. Fish pick at its once worshipped flesh. Around it lie scarab beetle sculptures, the devourers of the dead.

Come to me.

The voice in my head is louder now. She must be close.

The temple suddenly looms out of the dark, its massive pillars half buried in the silt. Behind it lies the cemetery where caskets of animal dead have been uncovered. Mummified ibis, their beaks like daggers, fragile bones crumbling as the air reached them. Perhaps this city was not meant to be found, after millennia under the sea.

A school of barracuda speed from the dark

and whirl about us, the flash of silver bodies making me dizzy. I sink to the bottom and kneel on the sea bed, perfectly still as I look up at them. Their beady eyes gaze down, assessing potential prey, gulping at the water with strong jaws and razor teeth for ripping flesh apart. Perfect predators. There are sharks in the Mediterranean, but these fish are more terrifying. They hunt in packs and they outnumber us.

This is their domain.

My fists clench as they circle closer.

"Beautiful, aren't they?"

Khalid's voice is almost a shock in the quiet of the deep but the full face-masks make communication possible down here. Still, I don't want him intruding. I say nothing and stare up at the whirling fish.

After a moment, they pass on and I push up from the sea bed, finning towards the Temple.

A hand on my ankle tugs me back, fingers tight and bruising.

I spin and kick out at Khalid and turn to see him smile.

With the other hand, he runs his fingers up my leg. I struggle against him.

"Don't go too far." He squeezes once more and then lets me go. My heart hammers in my chest; my breath comes fast as I remember him pinning me down that night.

Is he worried that I might report him now it's the end of the season?

Could he leave me down here?

I swallow down the bile in my throat and fight to regain my composure. I can't afford to drain my air too fast. There's not enough time.

I take one more deep breath and let it out slowly before finning away, acutely aware of him behind me.

Then I know what I must do.

An ancient path winds past the temple colonnade and I swim along it, just above the sea floor. Suddenly, I give two powerful kicks, enough to disturb the thick silt, sending it in a plume in front of him, rendering him blind. I switch off my torch, turn sharp left and duck inside the temple.

The hall is half buried and the silt is thick in here, swept in by the storm and churned in the entrance way. Unable to see, a wave of vertigo sweeps over me and for a moment, I don't know which way is up or down or how to find my way out again.

Panic rises within.

"Lara, where are you? I was only playing. I'm sorry. Come back."

Khalid's voice anchors me. I can't let him find the Dark Queen or he'll claim the find.

It has to be me — alone.

I reach out my hand and find the carvings on the wall. The horns of the Apis bull orientate me and I pull myself around and down towards the opening I saw on my last dive.

But the silt has shifted and the entrance is too tight for me to swim through in full gear. I hesitate but if the storm continues, this might be my only chance. The temple could be buried again tomorrow.

There's only one way I can do this, but the thought makes my mouth dry and my head pound. Without a buddy, it's a huge risk.

I could be trapped in here … lose my air … drown in convulsions of agonized breath.

Help me, please.

The voice is loud in my head.

The Dark Queen is close, crushed beneath tons of silt for millennia, just waiting for me.

I pull off my BCD jacket with tank attached, keeping the regulator in my mouth. I swim into the shaft and pull the tank with one hand, a more streamlined shape now its bulk is behind me. I claw my way along the shaft, fingernails scraping on the stone. It goes on too long, too far, and the silt blinds me. Then, suddenly, the rock ends and I emerge into the inner chamber.

There's a palpable presence in here and for a moment, I don't want to turn on my torch. The dead have lain here alone for so long.

What if something else is here? What if it has been waiting?

Don't be crazy. This is your chance.

I switch my torch on, the beam turned down in case Khalid is in the outer temple. Then I see her, just a partial face emerging from the seabed, a gentle, generous smile playing around her lips, eyes unseeing as they gaze towards me. Even the tiny part of what I can see is beautiful.

I look at my dive computer. My air is low. We've been down too long, but I can't leave her now.

I scrabble at the silt around the statue, digging my fingers through the dirt that clutches her. Tiny shells slice at my flesh and blood seeps from my fingertips as I reach down through the layers of history.

Slowly, I uncover perfectly smooth skin. I touch the rise of her breasts, the silk of her dress, but her arms are still pinned. My breath comes faster now and I tear at the silt that covers her, clawing it away in great handfuls. The dust of the dead whirls in the water around me and I can hardly see now, but as I pull away the stone that crushes her arms, I see she is almost free.

The torch flickers, and her gentle smile turns cruel. Her smooth skin crumples into withered scars, diseased flesh dissolved by the ocean. The edges of a yellowed skull emerge with teeth bared in fury. I scream into my mask and push the dead thing away.

The torch light goes out.

A crushing pain around my chest as the weight of stone pins me to the bottom of the chamber, driving the air from my lungs.

Something brushes my face and my mask is swept off.

My regulator is gone. My air is gone.

I can't breathe.

Struggling against the weight of rock above, I scan the darkness with unseeing eyes. The salt stings and presses against my throat, urging me to inhale the dead city.

I try to stop myself but the weight presses down on my chest again and I can't help it.

I gasp. Water rushes in and I gag. Convulse.

Light explodes in my mind and I only wish it was over.

Then suddenly the weight is gone, the water is gone. I can breathe. It's as if I am born again. Oh, sweet breath. I open my eyes.

No, no. It can't be.

I'm looking at myself. I see my own face behind the dive mask. Another Lara looks back at me with a cruel smile.

A Dark Queen must always remain with the city, but each may call another to her place.

"Lara, where are you?"

Khalid's voice is worried. The glimmer of his torch pierces the gloom of the inner chamber and the Lara-who-is-not-me turns away. She drags the tank back down the tunnel towards him, leaving me in the dark, an effigy of a wronged woman.

Through the tunnel, I can just see her reach for Khalid and grasp his hand before the silt swirls around me, hiding them from sight.

"Let's go up now," she says softly. "I've been down here too long."

Her voice is my own, faint now as the two ascend together towards the silhouette of the boat far above.

The storm whips the seabed into a maelstrom of silt, filling the inner chamber as my tomb shifts and sinks once more.

AUTHOR'S NOTE

This story is based on the Sunken Egypt exhibition at the British Museum in 2016. The Dark Queen statue was brought up from the sunken city of Thonis-Heraklion.

You can see the images that inspired the story at:
www.Pinterest.com/jfpenn/sunken-egypt

The Dark Queen short story was first published in Feel The Fear anthology (Sept 2017) published by WMG Publishing.

ENJOYED THE STORIES?

Thanks for reading *The Dark Queen*. I hope you enjoyed the stories and a review on the store where you bought the book would be much appreciated.

If you'd like to try more of my books, you can get a free copy of my bestselling supernatural thriller, *Day of the Vikings*, when you sign up to join my Reader's Group.

You'll also be notified of giveaways, new releases, and receive personal updates from behind the scenes of my books.

WWW.JFPENN.COM/FREE

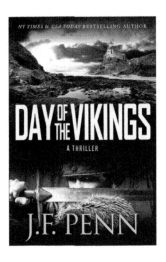

* * *

Day of the Vikings, an ARKANE thriller

A ritual murder on a remote island under the shifting skies of the aurora borealis.

A staff of power that can summon Ragnarok, the Viking apocalypse.

When Neo-Viking terrorists invade the British Museum in London to reclaim the staff of Skara Brae, ARKANE agent Dr. Morgan Sierra is trapped in the building along with hostages under mortal threat.

As the slaughter begins, Morgan works alongside psychic Blake Daniel to discern the past of the staff, dating back to islands invaded by the Vikings generations ago.

Can Morgan and Blake uncover the truth before Ragnarok is unleashed, consuming all in its wake?

Day of the Vikings is a fast-paced, supernatural thriller set in London and the islands of Orkney, Lindisfarne and Iona. Set in the present day, it resonates with the history and myth of the Vikings.

If you love an action-packed thriller,
you can get Day of the Vikings for free now:

WWW.JFPENN.COM/FREE

Day of the Vikings features Dr. Morgan Sierra from the
ARKANE thrillers, and Blake Daniel from the London
Crime Thrillers, but it is also a stand-alone novella that
can be read and enjoyed separately.

MORE BOOKS BY J.F.PENN

If you like **action adventure thrillers with a supernatural edge**, check out the **ARKANE** series as Morgan Sierra and Jake Timber solve supernatural mysteries around the world.

Stone of Fire #1
Crypt of Bone #2
Ark of Blood #3
One Day In Budapest #4
Day of the Vikings #5
Gates of Hell #6
One Day in New York #7
Destroyer of Worlds #8
End of Days #9
Valley of Dry Bones #10

Available in ebook, print, and audiobook editions as well as boxsets.

* * *

If you like **crime thrillers with an edge of the supernatural**, join Detective Jamie Brooke and museum researcher Blake Daniel, in the London crime thriller trilogy:

Desecration #1
Delirium #2
Deviance #3

Available in ebook, print, and audiobook
editions as well as boxsets.

* * *

If you enjoy **dark fantasy,** check out:

Map of Shadows, a Mapwalker novel #1
Risen Gods
American Demon Hunters: Sacrifice

A Thousand Fiendish Angels: Short stories based on
Dante's Inferno

The Dark Queen: An archaeological short story

More books coming soon.

If you loved the book and have a moment to spare,
I would really appreciate a short review on the page
where you bought the book. Your help in spreading
the word is gratefully appreciated and reviews make a
huge difference to helping new readers find the series.

Thank you!

ABOUT J.F.PENN

J.F.Penn is the Award-nominated, New York Times and USA Today bestselling author of the ARKANE supernatural thrillers, London Crime Thrillers, and the Mapwalker dark fantasy series, as well as other stand-alone stories.

Her books weave together ancient artifacts, relics of power, international locations and adventure with an edge of the supernatural. Joanna lives in Bath, England and enjoys a nice G&T.

*   *   *

You can sign up for a free thriller,
Day of the Vikings, and updates from behind the scenes, research, and giveaways at:

WWW.JFPENN.COM/FREE

* * *

Connect at:

www.JFPenn.com
joanna@JFPenn.com
www.Facebook.com/JFPennAuthor
www.Instagram.com/JFPennAuthor
www.Twitter.com/JFPennWriter

* * *

For writers:

Joanna's site, www.TheCreativePenn.com, helps people write, publish and market their books through articles, audio, video and online courses.

She writes non-fiction for authors under Joanna Penn and has an award-nominated podcast for writers, The Creative Penn Podcast.

Printed in Great Britain
by Amazon

27128132R00020